W9-AUD-896

DATE DUE

JUL 1 5 1998	JUN 1 8 2007		
JUL 2 4 1998			
JUL 3 0 1998			
JUN 1 7 1999			
JUL 10 '99			
AUG 0 6 1999			
JUN 1 3 2000			
AUG 0 2 2000			
JUN 2 8 2002			
AUG 1 6 2005			
APR 1 6 2007			

10.96

Goosebumps®

PRESENTS

It's creepy. It's spooky. It's funny . . . It's GOOSEBUMPS on Fox Kids TV!

Don't you love it? If you love the show, you'll love this book, *Attack of the Mutant*. It's exactly what you see on TV — complete with pages and pages of color photos from the show! It's spook-tacular!

So check under your bed, pull your covers up tight, and read *Attack of the Mutant*. GOOSEBUMPS PRESENTS is so good . . . it's scary!

Look for more books
in the GOOSEBUMPS PRESENTS series:

Goosebumps®

PRESENTS

ATTACK OF THE MUTANT

Adapted by Melinda Metz
From the teleplay by Billy Brown & Dan Angel
Based on the novel by R.L. Stine

SCHOLASTIC INC.
New York Toronto London Auckland Sydney

A PARACHUTE PRESS BOOK

Adapted by Melinda Metz, from the screenplay by Billy Brown and Dan Angel. Based on the novel by R.L. Stine.

ISBN 0-590-93969-6

Photos courtesy of Protocol Entertainment © 1996 by Protocol Entertainment.
Photos: Steve Wilkie
Text copyright © 1997 by Parachute Press, Inc.
All rights reserved. Published by Scholastic Inc.
GOOSEBUMPS is a registered trademark of Parachute Press, Inc.

12 11 10 9 8 7 6 5 4 3 2 1   7 8 9/9 0 1 2/0

Printed in the U.S.A.

First Scholastic printing, May 1997

ATTACK OF THE MUTANT

1

The evil Masked Mutant stalked across the rooftop. His blue cape flapped behind him. His extra-large muscles bulged with each step.

"I've come here to destroy you," the Mutant announced. The villain smiled at the Galloping Gazelle — the greatest superhero in The League of Good Guys.

"You're old, Gazelle," the Mutant growled. "Your hair is turning gray. And you're getting slow. You should start calling yourself the Trotting Turtle."

The Masked Mutant took a step forward. He gave a proud laugh as the old superhero backed away from him.

The Galloping Gazelle held his hands up in front of him, trying to keep the evil Mutant away. The Gazelle took another step back — until the heel of one of his yellow boots slipped off the roof. He glanced over his shoulder at the street far below.

"It's time to retire, Gazelle." The Mutant grinned his evil grin. *"Forever."*

He lunged at the Gazelle. One of his black leather gloves grabbed the old superhero's arm. But the Gazelle yanked his arm away.

WHOOSH! The Gazelle disappeared over the edge.

The Mutant gasped. His enemy had vanished. Where had he gone? The villain teetered on the edge of the roof. Then he fell. His blue cape flapped behind him as he tumbled over and over through the air.

"I still have a few years left," the Gazelle called from the side of the building. He clung there like a huge yellow and brown spider. "Thanks for *dropping* by, Mutant!"

The Gazelle stuck out his chin and grinned.

"Another victory over evil for The League of Good Guys!" he announced.

But as the Gazelle began to climb back up to the roof, something slimy and purple wrapped itself around his ankle. Then the head of a giant squid appeared next to him. A squid wearing a blue mask. The mask of the Masked Mutant!

It was the evil supervillain. He had changed into a squid!

The Galloping Gazelle screamed. He tried to yank his leg free. But another long, squishy, purple tentacle wrapped around the Gazelle's chest. And started to squeeze.

"I'll try not to leave any 'squid marks,'" the Masked Mutant snarled. His supersharp fangs sparkled in the sunlight.

The tentacles tightened around the Gazelle. Squeezing and squeezing and squeezing. The Gazelle's face twisted in pain.

"Skipper, Dad's home," he said.

Huh? I stared at my comic book.

"Skipper, Dad's home."

That wasn't the Galloping Gazelle speaking! That was Mom. I lowered the comic book and found her standing at the end of my bed. "I don't think you want your dad to see you reading that," she said.

I sat up. "But, Mom," I explained. "The Masked Mutant changed into a giant squid and he has the Galloping Gazelle in a death grip. I have to finish it. Pleeeeze?"

"Well . . ." Mom began.

"Skipper, is your homework done?" Dad asked as he walked into my room.

"Uh, not all of it," I admitted.

"Your grades are so poor because you spend all your time buried in a comic book," Dad told me. "You need a better hobby than reading that junk."

I stared up at my parents. Dad looked annoyed. And Mom seemed worried. Dad is almost always annoyed about something. And Mom is almost always worried.

"But I collect comic books," I tried to explain. I jumped up and grabbed one of the special first editions from the pile on my desk. I keep them wrapped in plastic. "Like this *Silver Swan*. Do you know how much this comic is worth?"

Dad sighed loudly. "That's not the point, Skipper. You don't pay attention to anything else." He turned to Mom. "He doesn't pay attention to anything else," he said.

I glanced down at the comic book on my lap. I began to read: "I'll try not to leave any 'squid marks,'" the Masked Mutant snarled."

"Skipper, try to pay attention to something else," I thought I heard Mom say. But she sounded far away. And the Gazelle was in real trouble.

"You see what I mean?" Dad hollered at her. "Skipper!"

"Huh? What?"

Dad snorted. He was really angry now.

Mom glanced at me. Then she glanced at Dad. She hates it when we argue. "It's dinnertime," she said nervously.

"Great!" I cried. I love Mom's cooking. I rushed toward the dining room. I wanted to eat quickly so I could get back to my comic and find out what happened to the Galloping Gazelle.

Would the Masked Mutant squeeze him to death? Would the most evil supervillain in history destroy the old superhero?

I didn't know it then, but the Galloping Gazelle wasn't the only one in danger from the Masked Mutant.

Not even close.

2

"Which one is the Masked Mutant again?" Wilson Clark asked at lunchtime the next day. Wilson is my best friend — but he doesn't know a thing about comic books.

"Which one? I can't believe you!" I shook my head. "The Mutant is the most evil comic book supervillain there is."

I pulled the latest Masked Mutant comic out of my backpack and handed it to Wilson. "Look. It's the first time they have ever shown the secret headquarters of the Mutant! In issue number twelve, page four, panel three, the Mutant *talks* about his headquarters. But they've never *shown* it before."

"Uh-huh," Wilson said. He used the comic book to swat a fly away from his face. Wilson and I like to eat at the tables outside Franklin Junior High.

I snatched my comic book back.

"*Uh-huh?* That's all you can say?" I cried. "The Mutant's headquarters is amazing. Look — the building is shaped like a huge fire hydrant. And it's twice as tall as anything around it." I pointed to the drawing. "Have you ever seen a pink and green building like this? It's the coolest."

"Uh-huh," Wilson said again. "Wait until you see the new rock I found." He threw his backpack on the table. It made a loud clunking sound. I rolled my eyes. Wilson doesn't carry books in his backpack. He carries rocks! He pulled one out — an ordinary gray rock.

Sometimes I can hardly believe I have a friend who collects something so dumb. Every day he wants to show me a new rock. I think they all look the same.

"What's so great about that one?" I asked.

Wilson cupped the rock in his hands. "If you hold it like this, it looks like a duck."

I stared at it. "It does?"

Wilson stared at it, too. "Well, it did this morning," he answered. "Hey, I'm going to go look for more rocks after school. Want to come?"

I shook my head. "I have to take the bus to the orthodontist." I will be so glad when I finally get these braces off, I thought. When you look at me all you see is braces, braces, and more braces.

Wilson pulled out another rock and placed it on the table.

I shivered. It wasn't cold out, but I felt a chill creep up my spine. I felt as if someone were staring at me.

I glanced at the big bush behind our table. The branches were blowing in the wind. Nobody was watching me. I turned back to Wilson. "How come you collect rocks, anyway?" I asked.

"I don't know," he answered. "They're easy to find. No matter where you are, you're always near a rock. I don't see what the big deal about comic books is."

"Are you nuts?" I cried. "Comic books are the greatest!"

Wilson unwrapped his sandwich. "I got tuna. What did you get?"

"Tuna," I answered.

"Want to trade?" he asked.

"What for?" I asked.

Wilson shrugged. "I don't know."

I laughed. "Okay." As I unwrapped Wilson's sandwich, I got that weird feeling again — as if someone were looking at me. I glanced over my shoulder. The bush was still blowing around. I didn't see anything strange.

"What's wrong?" Wilson asked.

"I don't know," I admitted. "I felt as if someone was watching me."

Wilson peered into the bushes and shook his head. "I don't see anything."

"I guess you're right," I said. "There isn't anyone there."

But the weird feeling didn't go away.

The Mutant's headquarters are amazing, I thought, as I read my comic on the bus to the orthodontist.

"Hey — do you go to Franklin?" a voice asked.

"Huh?" I mumbled. I was at a really good part — the Mutant was about to mutate again. But I forced myself to look up.

A girl sat across the aisle from me. She had long blond hair. I had never seen her at school.

"Me?" I asked.

"I wasn't talking to the empty seat." She smiled at me. Her teeth were straight. I always notice people's teeth.

I smiled back — with my mouth closed. I didn't want her to see my braces. "Uh, yeah. I go there . . . to Franklin."

"How is it?"

"Franklin?" I asked. "It's okay. It's an okay school."

The girl glanced at my comic book. "I didn't mean to interrupt your reading," she said.

"That's okay. I already read it four times,"

I told her. The back of my neck felt hot. It does that when I get embarrassed.

"Do you collect comic books? So do I. My name is Libby," she said all in a rush.

"What kind?" I asked.

"I collect *High School Harry and Beanhead*," she told me.

"Yuck! Those are the worst!" I cried.

Libby shook her head until her blond hair flew. "They're very well written. And they're funny. What do you collect?" she asked loudly. "All that superhero junk?"

"Junk!" I yelped. "My collection is worth about two thousand dollars. Your *High School Harry* comics are worth about two dollars!"

Libby shrugged. "I just like reading them." She leaned over and studied the cover of my comic. *"The Masked Mutant?"*

"I know everything about him," I bragged. "Everything. Even little things — like the Mutant always wears black gloves. And he can change himself into anything solid — but if he changes into a liquid, he's dead. Right now the Mutant is battling the Galloping Gazelle —"

"The *Gazelle*?" Libby giggled. "That's so dumb!"

"It's not dumb," I argued. "The Gazelle is battling the Mutant to save the planet. What's dumb about that?"

The bus hit a bump in the street. I glanced out the window. "Oh, man!" I cried. "I missed my stop." I stood up, grabbed my backpack, and stuck my comic book inside.

"See you around," I said to Libby. I hurried to the front of the bus. I got off at the next stop.

I jogged across the street to wait for another bus. I had never even *seen* this part of town before. No one was around. The buildings were all empty. It gave me the creeps. I hoped I wouldn't have to wait here too long.

I stared down the street, watching for the bus.

Wait. What was that? I leaned forward to get a better view.

My heart froze in my chest. Then it gave a hard thump.

No, I told myself. No way.

I squeezed my eyes shut, then slowly opened them. I stared down the street again.

"No," I whispered. "This is impossible!"

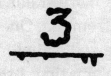

3

On the corner stood a huge building. A huge pink and green building shaped like a fire hydrant. It looked exactly like the Masked Mutant's secret headquarters!

I ran down the street to the building. I stared up at it. I had to tilt my head way back because it was so tall. At the top I could see a round green dome.

A shiver rushed through me. How could this be happening? "It's exactly like the drawing in my comic book," I whispered. "Exactly."

I had to look inside. I moved up to the front door. It was made of pink glass. I pressed my face against it. The glass felt cold against my forehead and nose. And it was covered with little crisscrossed scratches. It was hard to see through.

I jammed my face tighter against the glass. I wanted to see more. Four elevators lined the wall across from me. One was open, and light from inside spilled onto the lobby floor. Whoa! This is so amazing, I thought.

A shadow crossed in front of the open elevator. I jerked my head back. What was that? I wondered.

I reached for the door handle and turned it. It was unlocked! Should I go in? I swallowed hard.

I pushed the door open a crack. Then I heard the sound of an engine behind me — my bus was coming!

Oh, no! If I miss my orthodontist appointment I'll be in big trouble.

I glanced up at the building. "I'll be back," I whispered.

"It was the exact same building!" I told Wilson that night. We were hanging around in my room. We were supposed to be doing homework, but all I could think about was the Mutant's headquarters.

"I've got it!" Wilson cried. "I bet the guy who draws the Masked Mutant was in town one day." He began to walk up and down the length of my room. "And he drove down the street and saw that weird building. He decided it would be perfect for the secret headquarters of the Masked Mutant. So he drew it in the comic books!"

"I didn't think of that," I answered. "It makes sense." I felt sort of disappointed. It would be so cool if the Mutant's headquarters were real — and in my town.

Wilson stared at me. "You didn't really think it was the Mutant's headquarters, did you?" he asked.

"No," I lied. "But I still want to see it again."

My dad tapped on my door. "Time to go home, Wilson," he called. "It's getting late."

After Wilson left, I got ready for bed. But I couldn't fall asleep. I wanted to read. Just for

17

a little while. I had to find out what the Mutant was up to now.

I grabbed my penlight from under my pillow. Then I tiptoed over to my desk and picked up the latest *Mutant* comic book. I dove back in bed and made a little tent under the covers. That way no light could get out. Which meant Mom and Dad wouldn't know I was still awake.

I opened the comic book. The Masked Mutant stood at the control panel in his secret headquarters. He twisted a dial. "In control — and on a roll!" he cried.

I turned to the next page.

Suddenly a huge hand in a black glove grabbed my blankets.

It ripped the top off my tent.

My comic book fell from my hands.

"Aaaaaah!" I screamed.

4

Oh, no! I had seen that black glove before —
on the Masked Mutant! The Masked Mutant
ripped the covers off me!

I screamed again.

"Caught you!" Dad yelled.

He stood there in his raincoat with his
black driving gloves on. "I was just on my
way back from the store for your mother. I
had a feeling you would be awake."

I sat up in bed. "Sorry. I wanted to read a
little more."

Dad stared down at the book on my bed.
My math textbook.

"*Algebra?*" he said. "Skipper, I can't tell

you how happy I am to see you reading that."
Dad shook his head. "But go to sleep now.
And don't forget you have a follow-up ortho-
dontist appointment tomorrow."

"Okay. Good night," I said. The second he
left I opened my algebra book.

I had slipped my Mutant comic inside so
Dad wouldn't see it.

I stared down at the drawing of the headquarters. I couldn't wait to see that place
again. And I knew the perfect time — right
before my orthodontist appointment tomorrow!

The next day, I didn't read on the bus. I
was too excited about seeing the Mutant's
headquarters again. When the bus pulled
over to the curb, I bounded down the steps
and out the door.

I ran down the block to the headquarters.
But all I found was an empty lot.

"No way!" I yelled. I looked across the
street. I turned around and stared in all
directions.

But the Mutant's headquarters were gone. The huge pink and green building had disappeared. Disappeared!

An old man slowly walked past me. "Excuse me," I called. "Wasn't there a building here? It looked just like this drawing." I pointed to my comic book.

"Never noticed it," he answered.

"How could you *not* notice such a huge building?" I asked.

"I guess because it isn't there," he snapped. "No wonder you're imagining things. Why don't you try reading a good book instead of that junk."

Did I mess up? Was I in the wrong place?

I gazed around at the deserted buildings. No, this is right where I was yesterday, I thought.

I stared at the empty lot. I know the Mutant's headquarters were here yesterday, I thought. I know it.

"Hi, Mom," I called as I walked into the kitchen.

She jumped in surprise. She was reading a romance book — she loves them as much as I love my comic books. "Hi, sweetie. How was the orthodontist?" she asked.

"Same as always," I answered. What can you say about some guy poking around in your mouth?

"Oh, you have some mail," Mom told me.

She handed me a comic book wrapped in brown paper. The words SPECIAL EDITION were stamped on the front of it. "Huh? I've never gotten a comic in the mail before," I muttered.

I tore off the paper — and sucked in my breath. The headline on the front cover read MASKED MUTANT'S HEADQUARTERS VANISH!

Vanish. Just the way the pink and green building did yesterday.

I gasped.

My comic book was coming true!

The next day after school, I rushed straight to the empty lot where I'd seen the Mutant's headquarters. After I read the special edition comic book, I knew I had to go back right away.

Footsteps pounded up behind me. A deep voice boomed, "Attack of the Mutant!"

I gasped and spun around.

Libby. The girl I met on the bus. She was grinning at me. "I got you good," she teased.

"It's not funny," I snapped. I held out my new comic book and pointed to a picture of the Mutant's secret headquarters. "That building was right here the other day."

"I've never seen it," Libby said.

"Well, I have. And last night I got this in the mail." I flipped through the comic until I found the right page. It showed the Mutant in a control room filled with TV monitors. Each monitor showed a superhero from The League of Good Guys.

"So?" Libby said.

"Did you read what the Mutant is saying?" I asked. "He's thrown an Invisibility Curtain around his headquarters!"

"And you think that's why there isn't a building in this lot? Because of an Invisibility

Curtain." She shook her head. Her blond hair whipped around her face. "Now I know why they call you Skipper. When they handed out brains, you got skipped!"

I ignored her joke. "You have to admit it's weird," I said.

"I'll admit *you're* weird," she teased.

I kept staring at the lot. "In the comic book, people just stepped through the Invisibility Curtain. Once they were through it, they could see the building."

Libby grabbed my arm. "Okay. Let's get this over with. We are now stepping through the Invisibility Curtain," she said in a low, scary voice.

She gave my arm a tug.

We stepped forward.

I felt a cool mist cover my body.

I couldn't breathe.

Everything looked gray and fuzzy.

Then the mist cleared, and the pink and green building appeared!

"You . . . you were right!" Libby gasped. "It's here!"

24

"Let's go in!" I cried.

"Go in? Are you nuts?" she shouted.

"We have to. We have to find out if this is really the Mutant's headquarters." I pulled open the pink glass door and hurried inside. Libby followed me.

The lobby was huge. Maybe bigger than a football field. It was painted in bright neon colors. "Wow," I whispered.

I took a step forward.

BEEP!

A beam of yellow light shot out of the wall and ran down my body.

The hair on my neck stood up, and my skin felt all tingly.

"What was *that*?" I exclaimed.

"What?" Libby asked.

"Some kind of electric beam shined on me when I stepped forward. It felt really strange."

"I didn't feel anything," Libby said. "Are you trying to scare me or something?"

"No," I told her. "It — it was just weird. That's all."

I took a few more steps into the lobby.

My heart beat faster and faster as I glanced around.

"I know what you're thinking," Libby told me. "You think this really *is* the secret headquarters of that Mighty Mutator."

"The Masked Mutant," I corrected her. "And it must be his headquarters! How else do you explain the Invisibility Curtain?"

"I can't. It's weird," Libby answered. "It's *too* weird."

I started toward the open elevator. "There's only one way to find out the truth," I said.

"No way!" Libby cried.

I turned back to face her. "You can go home if you want to. But I'm going to ride that elevator to the top and see what's up there."

"All right. I'll come with you," Libby said.

I hurried into the elevator. I didn't want to give Libby a chance to change her mind. I was trying to act tough. But I really didn't feel like wandering through the Mutant's headquarters alone.

"If that Mutant creep shows up, I'm out of here," Libby warned me.

The elevator door closed. "I thought you didn't believe the Mutant was real," I said.

"I don't!" Libby insisted. But she didn't sound too sure.

I reached out and pressed the top button. "Here we go!" I whispered.

The elevator jerked. I heard a high whining sound.

"Hey! We're going down!" Libby yelled.

"We're going down — fast," I screamed. "Too fast!"

The elevator plunged down, down, down.

I grabbed the handrail tightly and screamed. "We're going to crash!"

5

I squeezed my eyes shut tight.

The elevator whooshed down faster and faster.

THUD! It suddenly slammed to a stop.

I fell and knocked my head on the wall. I looked over at Libby. "Are you okay?"

"I think so. Are you?" she asked.

"Yeah." I used the handrail to pull myself to my feet. "I don't get it. I pushed *up*. We should have gone *up*."

"Why isn't the door opening?" Libby stared at the closed elevator door. She glanced at me with a worried frown. "Skipper? Why isn't it opening?"

I pushed the DOOR OPEN button.

Nothing happened.

"Open!" I ordered.

The door didn't move.

"We're trapped in here," Libby moaned.

"No, we aren't. The door is just slow." I tried to convince her — and myself. "It will open. Watch."

We stared at the door.

It stayed closed.

"We'll be trapped in here forever!" Libby's voice grew higher and higher. "The air will run out! I can't breathe! I can't —"

The door slid open with a hiss.

"Oh," Libby said. Her face turned red.

I leaned out of the elevator. I saw a long, dark hallway.

"Where are we?" Libby asked.

I tried to see into the darkness. "The basement, I guess."

"Let's go back now," Libby said.

I could tell Libby was really scared. This place gave me the creeps, too.

I stepped back into the elevator and pushed the button marked LOBBY.

Nothing happened.

"Maybe we should get out and find another elevator," Libby suggested.

"Good idea," I said. We rushed into the hallway.

CLICK! The elevator door shut behind us. "No!" I yelled.

I pounded on the door with both fists. It didn't do any good.

Libby slowly started down the hall. "I don't see any other elevators — do you?" she asked.

I inched my way past her in the dark. "I can hardly see *anything*! Maybe the other elevators don't come all the way down here."

PHOWAAMMP!

I jumped.

"What was that noise?" Libby cried.

"I think it was the furnace," I said. "Come on. Maybe we can find some stairs. There has to be another way out of here." I stumbled forward a few steps. "Do you see any stairs, Libby?" I asked.

No answer.

"Libby? Where are you?"

I spun around.

Libby was gone. My throat went dry. Where is she? What happened to her?

"Libby!" I yelled again.

I ran down the dark hall searching for Libby.

I saw a thin strip of light coming from under a door. Maybe Libby went in there, I thought. I opened the door.

The room inside was empty — and totally white: the floor, the walls, the ceiling. Everything!

I turned to go.

Then I noticed a big drawing table in the far corner. The table was covered with brightly colored folders. I walked over and opened the red folder. A thin piece of paper fluttered out onto the desktop.

"Whoa," I gasped.

A drawing of the Masked Mutant stared up at me. So real, I felt as if he could actually see me.

I picked up a green folder off the table and

flipped through it. It was filled with drawings of superheroes — the Galloping Gazelle, with his yellow and brown suit. And all the others from The League of Good Guys. Plus drawing after drawing of the Masked Mutant.

"This must be where they make the comic books," I whispered.

I grabbed another folder and opened it.

"No way!" I cried.

Inside the folder was another stack of drawings. Drawings of *me*.

It's not me, I thought. That's impossible. I bent closer to the drawing. The boy had braces just like mine. He wore a striped T-shirt just like mine. His baseball cap looked just like mine.

It's me, I thought. I don't know how, but it is.

I heard something moving behind me. I spun around and stared at the door.

"Libby? Is that you?" I called. "Libby?"

Something rushed toward me from the

dark hallway. Something much too big to be Libby.

A pair of glowing red eyes appeared. Then a flowing blue cape.

The Masked Mutant!

His lips curled in an evil grin. Then he charged at me!

6

"Nooo! Nooo! Please . . . please don't — !" I cried as he closed in on me.

"Don't what?" a voice asked. A *familiar* voice.

"Got you!" Libby popped out from behind the Mutant and grinned at me. "It's only a big cardboard cutout." She laughed.

"Where did you find that?" I asked.

"Down one of the hallways. I found another elevator, too. Now we can get out of here."

"Wait. I have to show you something first." I led Libby over to the drawing table. "You won't believe it. I found some drawings of *me!*"

I turned to the table. It was empty.

The folders were gone.

"They were right here," I told Libby. "Right on this table!"

I checked under the table. I glanced around the white room. But the drawings of me were gone.

"Come on," Libby said. "We've fooled around down here long enough." She headed for the door.

"Libby, wait!"

But she didn't stop. So I followed her to the elevator and out of the building. I blinked as I stepped into the sunshine.

"I've got to get home. I'm so late. My mom is going to have a cow," Libby said.

"You don't believe me about the drawings, do you?" I asked.

"This whole thing is too weird for me," Libby replied. "See you around." She hurried off.

My bus pulled up across the street. I trotted toward it, but then I stopped. I just need one last look at the building, I thought. I turned around — and the building had disappeared.

I stared after Libby. She had disappeared, too.

"Is there something wrong with your spaghetti, dear?" Mom asked me at dinner that night.

I shoved a meatball around on my plate. "No. I'm just not that hungry," I told her. "The weirdest thing happened —"

"I heard something interesting on the radio when I was driving to work this morning," Dad interrupted.

I glanced over at him. Something was moving over his skin. What were those? Little bugs?

I stared harder.

Not bugs. Dots. Red, yellow, and blue dots! And they aren't moving over his skin, I realized. They *are* his skin.

It was like looking at a drawing of a comic book character up close. If you hold a comic right in front of your eyes, you can tell that the colors aren't solid. They are made of tons of little colored dots.

"A doctor said that some kids who read comic books have problems telling what's real from what's not," Dad said.

He kept talking as if nothing were wrong. Talking with lips made of red dots. Looking at me with eyes made of blue dots. "That's why I want you to have other interests," he told me.

I shook my head and glanced back over at my dad. He looked normal now. No dots.

"What were you about to say, Skipper?" Mom asked.

I couldn't remember. My head felt stuffy inside — the way it does when I have a cold. And there was a soft buzzing sound in my ears. So low, I could hardly hear it.

"I forgot," I mumbled. Maybe I'm getting a fever, I thought. That could explain why I was seeing things.

Or I'm going crazy — like the kids Dad was talking about.

* * *

That night I sat in my room trying to do my homework. But I couldn't. I kept thinking about the strange pink and green building that appeared and disappeared. And how for a minute I thought my dad was made out of dots.

And how some kids who read too many comic books couldn't tell what was real anymore. Was that happening to *me*?

"Skipper!" Dad called.

I jerked my head up. I didn't even hear him come in. I stared at Dad's face.

I swallowed hard.

Dad was changing again.

The dots were popping out all over his face.

I felt dizzy. I couldn't stand to look at him. I couldn't stand to look at all those yellow, red, and blue dots!

"One of your comic books came in the mail." He handed it to me. "But homework first, okay?"

I tried to nod. "Thanks, Dad."

He left my room, and I took a deep breath. Another comic in the mail.

Who was sending them to me? I almost felt afraid to look at it. But I ripped open the package.

Inside I found a *Masked Mutant* comic book. The words A NEW ENEMY FOR THE MUTANT were written across the top.

I opened the comic. My eyes widened in shock when I saw what was inside.

A drawing of *me* creeping down a dark hallway in the Mutant's headquarters.

I read the caption out loud. "'The boy sneaked down the hallway. At any moment he could be destroyed.'"

And I was the boy! I was *in* the comic book!

Everything in the comic book comes true, I thought. When the comic first showed the Masked Mutant's headquarters, I saw the headquarters. When the comic book said the Mutant's headquarters had an Invisibility Curtain, it did.

I couldn't believe it! Everything that happened in the comic was happening in *real* life!

And it was happening to me!

7

I tried to flip through the comic book — but my fingers wouldn't stop shaking.

The last page showed the Galloping Gazelle tied up in a tiny room. The furnace was on full blast — heating up the room like an oven. The Gazelle was sweating and turning red underneath his yellow and brown mask.

"'Two more minutes and I'll be a Grilled Gazelle,'" I read aloud. "'Only the boy can save me now. Only the boy can save me from the Masked Mutant's evil. But where is he?'"

I slammed the comic book shut. "Where is he?" I exclaimed. "I'm right here!"

I ran out of my room and tore into the kitchen with the comic book in my hand. "I'm in this comic book!" I shouted.

"You had a letter to the editor published?" Dad asked. He stood at the counter chopping onions.

"No!" I cried. I hurried over and held the comic open in front of him. "I'm *in* the comic book. That's me!"

Dad pushed the comic book away. "I can't see anything," he said. "The onions are making my eyes water."

"There is a trick to chopping onions," Mom said. "But I can't remember what it is." She sat at the table reading one of her romance books.

"Mom, you have to check this out," I pleaded. "I'm in here! It's really me!" I stuck the comic in front of her.

She glanced at it. "Yes, that does look a little like you," she answered. She went back to reading her book.

"Forget it," I muttered.

*   *   *

I stared up at the Mutant's headquarters and shivered. It looked different at night.

Maybe I should have waited until morning to come here, I thought. Maybe I should have tried harder to talk to my parents.

But I had to know if the story in the comic book was coming true.

I had to know if the Gazelle was inside, waiting for me to save him. So I sneaked out and took the bus back to the headquarters.

I pushed through the front door and crossed over to the elevators.

A low laugh filled the empty lobby.

I froze and listened.

I didn't hear it again. The building was silent.

An elevator stood open.

I stepped inside, but before I could push a button, the door slid shut. The elevator began to rise. I gripped my comic book tighter in my fist.

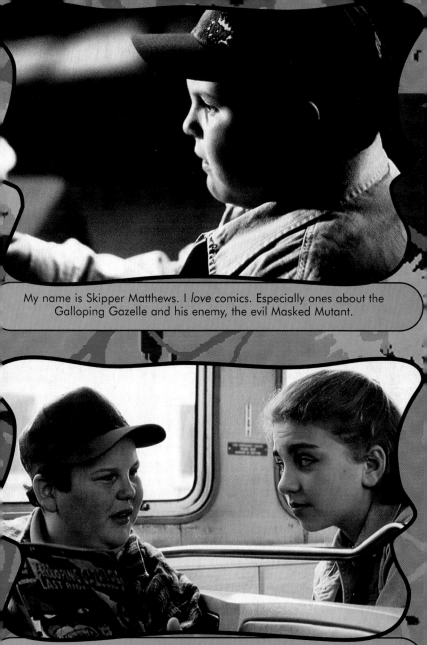

My name is Skipper Matthews. I *love* comics. Especially ones about the Galloping Gazelle and his enemy, the evil Masked Mutant.

One day on the bus, I met a girl named Libby. She was cool. But she made fun of my comics.

That day I missed my stop. When I got off the bus, I couldn't believe what I saw—a building that looked just like the Masked Mutant's headquarters in the comic book!

The next day I went back to check out the strange building. Libby came along.

We went inside to explore. We stepped into an elevator, and *WHOOOSH!* It dropped us to the basement.

Then the elevator wouldn't go back up. Libby and I were trapped in the creepy basement. We started searching all the rooms for a way out.

In one room I found drawings. Hey! This was where they made the Masked Mutant comic books, I realized. Then I saw something really amazing—drawings of *me*!

I turned around—and saw the Masked Mutant! Oh, no! I thought.
He's after me...

...I thought wrong. It was just Libby playing around with a cardboard
cutout.

The next night, I read my new comic under the covers. The Masked Mutant was about to destroy the world. Only the Galloping Gazelle could stop him. But he needed help—*my* help. Whoa! I *was* really in the comic book!

I had to help the Galloping Gazelle! I returned to the Masked Mutant's headquarters. I got there just in time to save him.

We still had to defeat the Masked Mutant. We sneaked into his control room.

But the Masked Mutant was too strong. He knocked out the Galloping Gazelle.

Now it was up to *me* to save the world from the evil Masked Mutant—but how?

What am I going to find up there? I wondered.

The elevator stopped. The door opened. I entered a hall painted with bright colors.

I opened my comic book — and saw a drawing of myself sneaking down *this* hallway. My knees started to shake. What was going to happen?

"Hello? Is anyone here? Hello?" I called.

THUMP! THUMP!

I moved toward the sound.

THUMP! THUMP! THUMP! It was coming from behind a door.

"Is anyone in there?" I called.

"Can you help me?" a faint voice answered.

I didn't know what to do. I didn't know who was behind that door.

"Please," the voice begged.

I slowly turned the doorknob. It felt warm under my hand. A blast of hot air blew out of the room as I pushed open the door — and saw the Galloping Gazelle!

He was tied to a chair. His face was sweaty

and red underneath his mask. I could tell the furnace was on full blast.

He glared at me. "Hey, kid." His voice sounded a lot louder on this side of the door. "What took you so long? Don't you know you have to help me save the world?"

"You — you're the Galloping Gazelle," I shouted. "You're real!"

"Yeah — *real* tired of waiting. Turn that heat off," the Gazelle snapped.

I spotted a huge red lever near the door. I reached up as high as I could and yanked it down.

"Now, untie me! We have to hurry," the Gazelle ordered.

"I can't believe this!" I couldn't stop staring at the Gazelle. He looked exactly the way he did in comic books. His muscles were huge, and —

"I'll give you my autograph later," the

Gazelle told me. "Hurry up. We don't have much time. The Mutant will be back."

"He will?" I asked.

"Yeah — and we want to get him before he gets us, right?" the Gazelle said.

"*Us?*" I repeated.

The Gazelle sighed. "You're the kid, right? You're the one who is going to help me fight the evil forces and save the planet, right?"

"I . . ."

The Gazelle shook his head. "What's your name?"

"Skipper," I said.

"Weird name for a superhero," the Gazelle muttered. "Just untie me, would you, kid?"

I knelt down next to the Gazelle's chair and started working on the big knots. My fingers were sweaty and they kept slipping.

"Hurry up," the Gazelle said. He stared closely at me. "How old are you anyway — eight, nine?"

I frowned at him. "I'm *twelve*!" I jerked on one of the knots, and the Gazelle pulled one arm free.

"Don't get an attitude," he told me. He raised his wrist communicator to his lips. "Come in, League of Good Guys. Come in, League of Good Guys."

No one answered.

"Oh, no!" the Gazelle exclaimed. "The Mutant must have jammed it."

I untied another knot. The Gazelle was almost free.

"How did you find the secret headquarters, anyway?" the Gazelle asked.

I used my teeth to loosen the next knot. "I . . . I just found it," I answered.

"Don't be modest," the Gazelle scolded me. "You read my thoughts and hurried to my rescue, right?"

"No. I took the bus."

I untied the last knot, and he sprang out of the chair. He stuck out his chin and gave his best superhero grin. "Now . . . let's go pay our friend a surprise visit."

"Where are we going?" I asked. But the Gazelle was gone!

I stared around the room — and found him

stuck to the ceiling! He moved so fast, I didn't even see him climb up there! "Coming?" he called.

"Can't we take the elevator?" I asked.

"No climbing abilities, huh? You know, if you're going to be a superhero, you have to start working out," the Gazelle said.

WHOOSH! A breeze blew through my hair — and the Gazelle was gone again. He must have sped up the stairs, I thought. I rushed out the door and over to the staircase.

I climbed as fast as I could, but when I reached the top, the Gazelle was waiting for me. "Take your time, take your time," he muttered. "We only have to save the planet."

I followed the Gazelle into the Masked Mutant's control room. Wow! It looked exactly the way it did in my comic book!

It had rows of television screens, and a long control panel covered with switches and buttons and dials. I wanted to try everything!

The Gazelle plopped down in the leather

swivel chair in front of the panel and stretched his legs out in front of him.

"This place is incredible!" I exclaimed.

"Eh," the Gazelle grunted. "It's not nearly as cool as the control room for The League of Good Guys. We have a soft drink machine!"

I suddenly remembered why we were here. "What are we going to do about the Masked Mutant?" I asked.

"We'll wait right here and surprise him," the Gazelle answered. He squirmed around. "I just wish this chair were more comfortable."

The Gazelle rubbed his hands over the black armrests — and long, scaly strips suddenly began to peel away.

Then the arms of the chair began to move! They began to ripple under his fingers!

"Look out, Gazelle!" I cried.

The arms of the chair were coming alive! They coiled around the Gazelle's arms — pinning him in place.

The chair was changing!

Shiny black eyes opened at the end of one armrest. A mouth stretched open wide. A long, forked tongue darted in and out. And venom dripped from a set of sharp yellow fangs.

The chair arms had turned into a huge snake!

I shrieked with terror.

The snake began to change again.

Its head bulged.

Its eyes turned red.

A blue mask appeared over the scaly black skin. It had changed into the Masked Mutant!

The Mutant was part-chair, part-snake, and part-supervillain — and he was totally evil!

He had the Galloping Gazelle trapped!

"What's wrong, Gazelle?" the Mutant asked. "Don't you like leather chairs? Well, how do you feel about snakeskin?"

The Mutant-chair-snake began to squeeze the Gazelle's chest. I stared around the room.

I had to save the Gazelle. What could I use as a weapon?

"Ssstick around," the Mutant-snake hissed. He grinned at me. "I'll squeeze us up some refreshing Gazelle juice."

"Agghhh," the Gazelle groaned. Then he winked at me. "Don't worry, kid. I've got an idea. Shall I give it a whirl?"

WHOOSH! The Gazelle turned into a huge whirlwind. He spun around so quickly that the Mutant-chair-snake began to turn with him.

It's going too fast! I realized.

BAM! The Mutant-chair-snake flew into the wall next to me. The Mutant changed back into his supervillain form.

I wanted to run away. But the Gazelle was still spinning. He looked like a tornado!

"Check out that windbag," the Mutant said. He nodded toward the Gazelle. Then he stuck his foot into the base of the whirlwind.

He tripped the spinning Gazelle!

THUNK! The Gazelle slammed against the

wall. He slid down it until he was sitting on the floor.

Then he stood back up and straightened his mask. He brushed off his tights. He pulled his belt around so the big buckle was in the front. "That's it. I'm out of here," he announced. He marched toward the door with his chin in the air.

"Wait!" I yelled. "Where are you going?"

"The Mutant was right," the Gazelle answered. "I *am* too old for this superhero stuff. You're on your own, kid."

WHOOSH! The Gazelle disappeared.

9

"Another victory for The League of *Scared* Guys," the Mutant said. He laughed. A mean laugh.

Then he turned toward me. His eyes glowed red.

"Aaah!" I screamed. I ran for the door — and crashed into Libby!

"Libby! Watch out! The Mutant —" I glanced over my shoulder. The Mutant was gone!

"Where did he go?" I cried.

The metal doors slid shut behind Libby. "Where did *who* go?" she asked. "Didn't you hear me call you? I was across the street when you came in here."

"Why are you out in the middle of the night?" I yelped.

"I knew you would come here tonight," Libby said. She wandered over to the control panel. "Wow. This is cool."

"Be careful!" I shouted. "He's in here. The Masked Mutant is in here. He could be that chair ... or that desk ..." I turned around and around, staring at everything in the room. "He could be the floor ... or the ceiling ... or ..."

"I know, I know," Libby teased. She rolled her eyes. "He's the Masked Mutant. He could be anything. He could even be *me*."

I stared at her. She stared back. She didn't smile.

My skin got that prickly feeling again. "That's not funny, Libby," I whispered.

She gave me a nasty grin. "There is no Libby," she said. "There never was."

Oh, no! Libby was the Masked Mutant!

As she walked toward me, her blond hair turned into the Mutant's blue helmet. Her thin arms stretched until they bulged with the Mutant's extra-large muscles.

She moved closer and closer. She grew taller. "And now I must do something very bad to you, Skipper." Her voice started out high and ended low and deep.

"But, why? I'll just leave and take the bus home. I won't tell anyone. Honest," I begged.

The Masked Mutant's eyes turned red. The change was complete.

I started to back away. But each time I took a step back, the Mutant took a step forward. "You belong here," he said. "I knew it the first time I saw you on the bus. I knew you were perfect when you said you knew everything about me."

"But . . . but . . ."

"It's so hard to find good characters for my stories," the Mutant continued. "It's so hard to find good enemies."

My back hit the wall. I had no way to escape.

The Mutant walked over to a six-foot-tall

machine. It was attached to a giant yellow anchor hanging from the ceiling. He polished it with his sleeve. "When you recognized my headquarters, I knew you were ready to star in a story."

He smiled at me. Then his smile faded. "I'm sorry, Skipper. Your story is over now."

The Mutant pushed a button. The machine made a horrible grinding sound.

Then the giant anchor began to move — toward me!

"W-what are you going to do?" I asked.

"I'm going to destroy you, of course!" The Mutant laughed. The anchor kept moving. The grinding sound made my heart pound.

I wanted to close my eyes and pretend this whole thing wasn't happening.

But I couldn't.

The huge yellow anchor hung right over my head.

The Mutant was going to drop it on me! I had to come up with a plan — fast!

"You can't destroy me!" I yelled. "You are

just a character in a comic book! But I'm real! I am a real, live person!"

The Mutant shook his head and made a *tsk-tsk* sound with his tongue. "No, you aren't, Skipper. You aren't real. You are a comic book character, too."

What? I ran my hands over my face. I ruffled up my hair. I pinched myself. I felt the same as always. "You're a liar!"

The Mutant threw back his head and laughed. "Remember when you entered the building for the first time? Remember when the beam of light passed over you?"

"Yeah . . . I remember." I tried not to sound scared.

"That was a scanner," the Mutant explained. "It scanned your body. It turned you into tiny dots of ink."

"No!" I shouted.

"That's all you are now," the Mutant said, his voice calm. "Tiny dots of red, blue, and yellow ink. You're a comic book character, just like me."

The yellow machine jerked into motion. It was going to crush me! "Now, say good-bye, Skipper," the Mutant cried.

"Wait!" I yelled. "I'm not Skipper. There never was a Skipper."

The Mutant rolled his eyes. "Oh, really? Then who are you?"

I stood up straight and stuck my chest out. I put my hands on my hips and gave him my best superhero grin.

"I'm . . . I'm . . . Elastic Boy!" I blurted out.

"Elastic Boy!" the Mutant exclaimed. "I thought you looked familiar."

I made my voice as low as I could. "Good-bye, Mutant. I have to go back to my home planet of, um, Zargos. I'm not allowed to guest-star in other comic books."

"Nice try, Elastic Boy," the Mutant said. "But you have invaded my secret headquarters. I must destroy you."

"Ha-ha! You cannot destroy Elastic Boy!" I bragged. "There is only one way that Elastic Boy can be destroyed."

"What is that, if you don't mind my asking?" The Mutant gave me a polite smile.

It's working! I thought. He's falling for my trick!

"Sulfuric acid," I declared in my Elastic Boy voice. "That's the only thing that can destroy my elastic body." Then I gasped in fake horror, "Oops! I didn't mean to let that slip out!"

"Too late. Say good-bye, Elastic Boy!" The Mutant's body turned into a shaking mass of jelly. Then it melted into a pool of bubbling green liquid — with the Masked Mutant's head on top. He was mutating into sulfuric acid!

I crouched down next to the smoking green pool. I stared into the Mutant's red eyes. "You forgot one thing, Mutant," I said. "You can change into anything solid and back again, but once you change into liquid, you're dead."

The Mutant howled in fury. "You tricked me! The great Masked Mutant tricked by a boy! Aaaghhh!"

The Mutant's head melted into the green puddle. All that was left of him was his mask.

I rolled up my comic book and fished the mask out of the sulfuric acid. "Yes!" I cried. "I have destroyed him! The most evil supervillain to ever walk the planet is dead!"

10

"You're not eating again, Skipper?" Mom asked the next day.

I tried to swallow a spoonful of soup, but the smell made me gag. "No, I'm not hungry," I answered.

Mom got up from the table. "I forgot to give you your mail."

"If it's a comic book, you can throw it out," I said quickly. I had dumped all my comics in the garbage when I got home from the Mutant's headquarters the night before. I never wanted to see another comic book as long as I lived!

But Mom handed me the brown-wrapped package, anyway.

"What's that on your hand?" she asked, frowning at me. "It looks like ink!"

"Don't worry, Mom. I won't get any on the furniture."

But Mom dragged me over to the sink, anyway. She turned on the water and began scrubbing my hand.

Forget it, I thought. That ink will never come off.

I wandered into the living room and plopped down on the sofa. I flicked on the TV.

Everything on the screen appeared to be made of yellow, red, and blue dots. The whole living room, too. And my mom. I saw everything in dots now.

Mom was still scrubbing my hand at the kitchen sink.

Suddenly I heard a scream. She must have noticed that I wasn't in the kitchen anymore.

My arm had stretched from the sink through the doorway — and all the way into the living room!

Mom gave another shriek and let go of my hand.

BOING! It sprang back into place.

Mom was still screaming.

I glanced at the comic that had been mailed to me. The cover read, EDITION #1: ELASTIC BOY.

I studied the picture underneath the title. The picture of *me*. "Cool!" I cried. "I'm streeeeetchin'!"

Hey Goosebumps fans!
Don't write this one off!

Boo dudes!
More greetings from the world of Goosebumps!
I've got a brand-new
collection of 30 totally
terrifying cards in The
Goosebumps® Postcard Book II —
with a different, scary Goosebumps
cover on the front of each one!

Collect 'em, swap 'em,
or send them to your
favorite monster.

Yours ghoully,
Curly

TO:

The
Goosebumps®
Postcard Book II

Coming this April to a bookstore near you.